⁹/₂₁

Dear Parents:

Congratulations! Your child is taking the first steps on an exciting journey. The destination? Independent reading!

STEP INTO READING® will help your child get there. The program offers five steps to reading success. Each step includes fun stories and colorful art or photographs. In addition to original fiction and books with favorite characters, there are Step into Reading Non-Fiction Readers, Phonics Readers and Boxed Sets, Sticker Readers, and Comic Readers—a complete literacy program with something to interest every child.

Learning to Read, Step by Step! DISCARD

Ready to Read   Preschool–Kindergarten
• **big type and easy words** • **rhyme and rhythm** • **picture clues**
For children who know the alphabet and are eager to begin reading.

Reading with Help   Preschool–Grade 1
• **basic vocabulary** • **short sentences** • **simple stories**
For children who recognize familiar words and sound out new words with help.

Reading on Your Own   Grades 1–3
• **engaging characters** • **easy-to-follow plots** • **popular topics**
For children who are ready to read on their own.

Reading Paragraphs   Grades 2–3
• **challenging vocabulary** • **short paragraphs** • **exciting stories**
For newly independent readers who read simple sentences with confidence.

Ready for Chapters   Grades 2–4
• **chapters** • **longer paragraphs** • **full-color art**
For children who want to take the plunge into chapter books but still like colorful pictures.

STEP INTO READING® is designed to give every child a successful reading experience. The grade levels are only guides; children will progress through the steps at their own speed, developing confidence in their reading.

Remember, a lifetime love of reading starts with a single step!

Published in the United States by Random House Children's Books, a division of Penguin
Random House LLC, 1745 Broadway, New York, NY 10019, and in Canada by Penguin Random
House Canada Limited, Toronto.

Step into Reading, Random House, and the Random House colophon are registered trademarks
of Penguin Random House LLC.

Visit us on the Web!
StepIntoReading.com
rhcbooks.com

Educators and librarians, for a variety of teaching tools, visit us at RHTeachersLibrarians.com

ISBN 978-0-593-30433-4 (trade) — ISBN 978-0-593-30434-1 (lib. bdg.)
ISBN 978-0-593-30435-8 (ebook)

Printed in the United States of America   10 9 8 7 6 5 4 3 2 1

WONDER WOMAN™

Wonder Woman Saves the Trees!

by Christy Webster

illustrated by Pernille Ørum

Wonder Woman created by
William Moulton Marston

Random House 🏠 New York

Wonder Woman
loves the Earth.

Wonder Woman grew up
on an island.
It was a beautiful place.
She played in forests.
She swam in the sea.

Now Wonder Woman
is a Super Hero.
She helps people.
She protects all creatures,
great and small, from
threats like Poison Ivy.

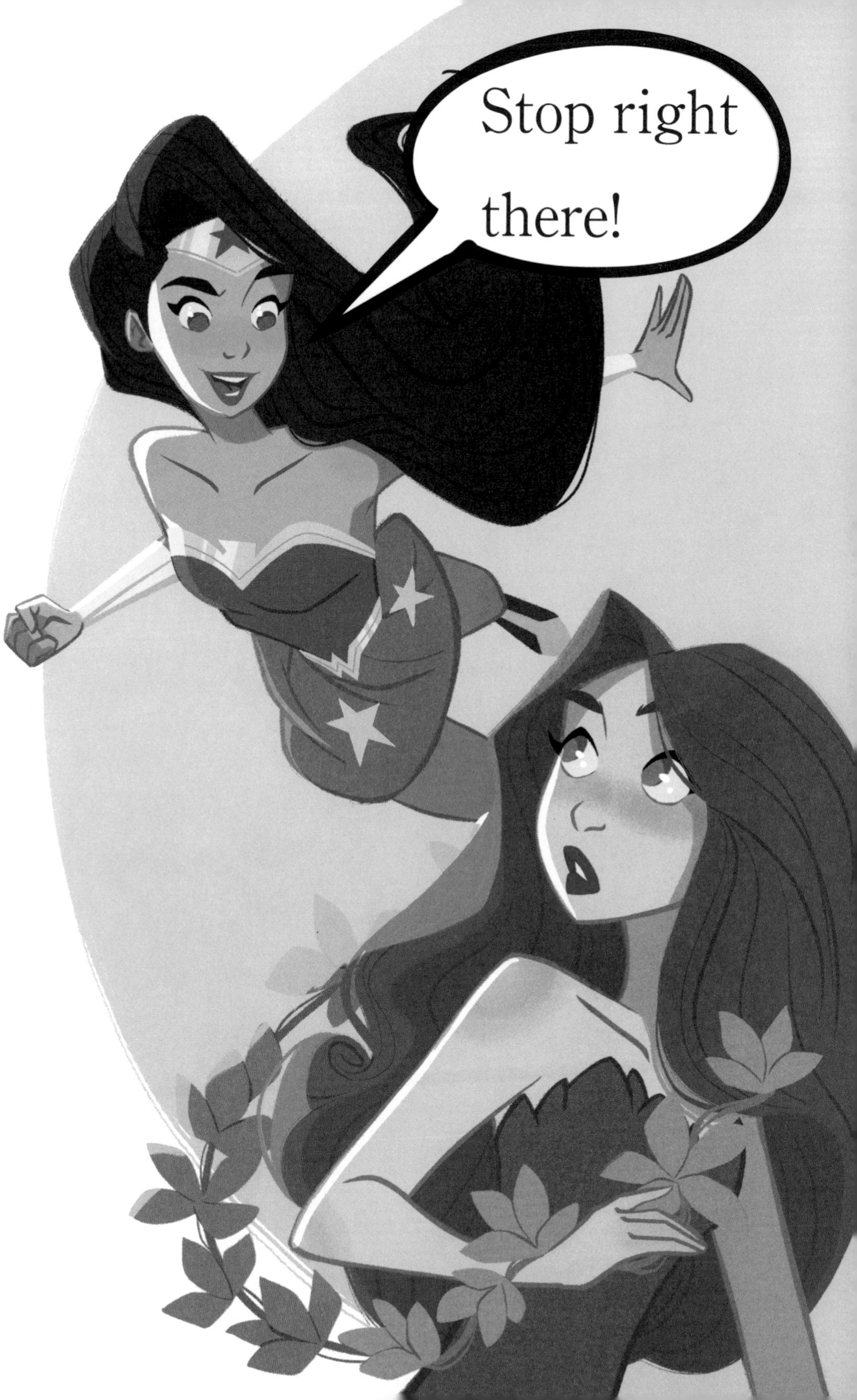
Stop right there!

Poison Ivy
loves the Earth, too.
But she is angry.
"They are cutting down
all the trees!"
she shouts.

Poison Ivy wants trees
to grow.
She does not like it
when people cut
them down.

Wonder Woman
talks to Poison Ivy
about working together
to help, not harm.
They go to the forest.
Many trees are gone.

Wonder Woman
gets started.
Poison Ivy joins her.
They clean up.

They plant new trees.

Other people start to help.

They clean the ocean.

They water the trees.

They work together.

Poison Ivy uses
her powers to help
the trees grow.
But you don't need
superpowers to plant
and water!

They help
the animals
find new homes.

If we all work together,
we can save the world.
Heroes love the Earth.
Heroes help the Earth!